First published in France under the title *Asticots* © Éditions Milan, 2010.

Text and illustrations © 2010 Éditions Milan
English translation © 2015 Kids Can Press
English translation by Yvette Ghione

Kids Can Press acknowledges the financial support of the Government of Ontario, through the Ontario Media Development Corporation's Ontario Book Initiative.

Published in Canada by
Kids Can Press Ltd.
25 Dockside Drive
Toronto, ON M5A 0B5

Published in the U.S. by
Kids Can Press Ltd.
2250 Military Road
Tonawanda, NY 14150

www.kidscanpress.com

The text is set in ITC Galliard.

English edition edited by Yvette Ghione

This book is smyth sewn casebound.
Manufactured in Malaysia in 3/2015 by Tien Wah Press (Pte.) Ltd.

CM 15 0 9 8 7 6 5 4 3 2 1

Library and Archives Canada Cataloguing in Publication

Friot, Bernard, 1951–
[Asticots. English]

1575

        Worms / written by Bernard Friot ; illustrated by Aurélie Guillerey ;
English translation by Yvette Ghione.

Translation of: Asticots.
ISBN 978-1-77138-571-8 (bound)

        I. Guillerey, Aurélie, illustrator II. Ghione, Yvette, translator III. Title.
IV. Title: Asticots. English.

PZ7.F8697Ast 2015   j843'.914   C2015-900466-7

Kids Can Press is a *lorus*™ Entertainment company

Worms

BY **BERNARD FRIOT**

ILLUSTRATED BY **AURÉLIE GUILLEREY**

KIDS CAN PRESS

I was bored. SO bored!

My father had invited the senior executives from the factory to dinner and made me join them.

He introduced me to everyone by saying, "And this is your future boss!" Because he owns the factory, and wants me to take it over one day.

I thought I might die of boredom before dinner was even served. They were all talking about things that were too boring for me to understand. So I was happy to help when my father asked me to bring in the salads. I had been trying so hard to sit still for so long, both of my legs had fallen asleep.

Everything was laid out on a serving cart in the kitchen. There was a crystal bowl for each guest filled with leafy salad, shrimp and a sprinkling of slivered almonds.

I'm not sure why, but looking at the salads, I suddenly thought of worms. The worms I use for fishing bait that I keep in the fridge, way at the back, behind the yogurt.

I got the jar out of the fridge, unscrewed the lid and
put one worm in each of the salad bowls.

Then I rolled the cart out into the dining room, served the salads and sat down.

After that, I wasn't bored anymore. I couldn't wait to see how everyone would react to the worms. They were all very interesting to watch. Except for Papa. He didn't stop talking. He devoured his salad, and the worm, without even noticing!

Ms. DeLuca nearly choked when she spied the sweet little worm wriggling next to her shrimp.

But she was sneaky. She looked right, then left, then — *PFFFT!* With a flick of her knife, she flung the worm as far as she could across the room.

No one suspected a thing.

Mr. Lopez really impressed me. When he discovered the squirmy intruder, he barely raised an eyebrow. He carefully wrapped the worm in a lettuce leaf and swallowed it whole.

Mr. Turner was the funniest. When he saw the worm, he hiccuped so hard, his glasses fell into his salad bowl. He fished them out and perched them on his nose, and then stared at the poor worm as though he was terrified it would eat him.

So I gave him a little encouragement.

"Don't you like shrimp, Mr. Turner?" I asked.

"Yes, yes … I mean, no … I mean, yes … yes, of course …" he stammered. And then, bravely, he picked up his fork and swallowed the worm in one bite, along with a big hunk of bread, which he forced down with a full glass of water.

Oh, the faces he made!

I was laughing so hard, I had to hide behind my napkin.
But then my father put a quick stop to my giggling.

"John-Paul, hurry up and eat.
Everyone else finished ages ago."

He used his bossy president voice. So I didn't argue.
In three forkfuls, I ate my salad ...

And — GULP! — the worm.